W9-AVS-966

This edition published by Parragon Books Ltd 2015

Parragon Inc.
440 Park Avenue South, 13th Floor
New York, NY 10016
www.parragon.com

Copyright © Parragon Books Ltd 2012 – 2015

Written by Claire Freedman   Illustrated by Russell Julian
Edited by Laura Baker   Designed by Kaye Hunter
Production by Jonathan Wakeham

All rights reserved. No part of this publication may be reproduced,
stored in a retrieval system or transmitted, in any form or by any means,
electronic, mechanical, photocopying, recording or otherwise, without
the prior permission of the copyright holder.

ISBN 978-1-4748-1034-0

Printed in China

Scaredy
BOO!

PaRragon

Bath • New York • Cologne • Melbourne • Delhi
Hong Kong • Shenzhen • Singapore • Amsterdam

Under the bed lived a monster,
A monster named **Scaredy Boo**.
Boo was afraid of everything.
He would have been scared of you!

Each night, the other small monsters
Raced around the house having fun.
Though all the children were sleeping,
Boo feared they'd **WAKE UP** someone!

Boo sighed, "I'm frightened of **Big** Things.
Small Things and Wiggly Things, too!
I'm little **Scaredy Boo** monster.
Wouldn't these things scare **YOU?**"

Scaredy Boo didn't like noises,
Things that went crackle or *squeak*.
Hearing strange whispers and rustles
Made poor Boo's legs go all weak!

Boo was afraid of things *Tickly*,
Things that had Big Furry Ears,
Things that had noses all Twitchy—
These were Boo's worst monster fears!

Late one night, Boo heard **loud** footsteps.
"**Help!** Something's out there!" he said.
"Hello," the Thing called. "You hiding?"
It peeked at Boo under the bed.

Scaredy Boo trembled, "Who are you?
I jump when someone shouts BOO!
I'm little Scaredy Boo monster.
Wouldn't YOU be scared, too?"